MW01095058

Squishmas

in

Squishville

Taira Foo

Illustrated by

Ann Foo

TAIRA

FOO

BOOKS

ESTABLISHED 2017

Dedicated to all the believers out there...

Contents

Squishmas in Squishville

Welcome to Squishville

Welcome to Squishville! Grandpa Squish and Grandma Squash live here. These funny little squirrels enjoy telling stories to all their little grandsquirrels and their friends. These tiny squirrels are called Squishes and Squashes.

Squishville is a really special place because it is made up of mushroom houses, each one with different-shaped spots just like a giraffe. Many marvellous characters live here and you will get to meet them all as you read all their magical stories.

1

I am going to introduce you now to a teeny tiny little Squish called Tiddlypops. Tiddlypops loves Grandpa Squish's stories so much he writes them down as soon as he gets home so doesn't forget them. When Tiddlypops grows up he wants to be just like Grandpa Squish.

Here he is...

Hello Everyone!

Say hello to Tiddlypops

My name is Tiddlypops and I live in a ginormous place called Squishville where everything is gigantic, including my best friend, Squatipops..

My favourite time in Squishville is when Grandpa Squish tells his stories to all us little Squishes and Squashes. I am always the first Squish to arrive at story time and the last to leave. I think Grandpa Squish is the cleverest squirrel ever because he knows so many things. Sometimes I get a bit annoyed at my friends because they start talking when Grandpa Squish is trying to tell his story, especially Sweet Pea. Sometimes she blurts things out and stops the story because she can't control her emotions.

Actually, Sausage Pot does that a bit too, especially if Grandpa Squish mentions anything to do with food. My best friend is Squatipops, which some of you might find strange because he is huge and I am tiny, but it doesn't matter to me or him because we are the best of friends.

I hope you're ready for story time tonight – I am so excited that I am going to leave extra early.

See you there!

Chapter One

The Squish & Pop Dance

Thank you, Tiddlypops.

It was Squishmas time in the land of Squishville and the magic had landed on this most enchanted of places. It was covered in a light fluffy snow and the sparkles were so bright you needed to put on an extra big pair of sunglasses to see where you were going.

Squishmas time in the land of Squishville

Just to add to all the excitement, Grandma Squash had started to grow Sparkle Stars in her garden, as she did every year.

The stars grew so big that they couldn't fit in the ground anymore and would eventually pop out, making a pinging noise that sounded a little bit like a caterpillar playing a tambourine. The Sparkle Stars giggled as they flew up to the tops of the mushroom -shaped houses, slid down the sides of the ever-so-spongy mushroom roofs, finding their way into Grandma Squash's secret mushroom soup.

This very special recipe was called Wishy Squishy Soup because the tiny, gold giggling Sparkle Stars would ask the little Squishes and Squashes to make a wish. This only happened once a year on Squishmas Eve. Once the little squirrels made their wishes, the Sparkle Stars would float up quicker than a rocket into the sky and begin to make all the little squirrels' wishes come true. However, one year there was one little Squish whose wish nearly didn't come true and that's the story Grandpa Squish is going to tell at story time tonight.

There were squibbles and squabbles and wibbles and wobbles

As the little Squishes and Squashes burst into Grandpa Squish and Grandma Squash's red mushroom house there were squibbles and squabbles and wibbles and wobbles. This was supposed to be the most wonderful time of the year, but instead it was turning into a wild and wacky circus without the fun. A little Squish called Sweet Pea decided that there was only one thing for it: the Squish and Pop dance. She knew that this would be the only way to calm the little squirrels down. With a big thud she placed her green spotty satchel, which was covered in lashings of glitter, next to the Squishmas tree. She placed her tiny paws on her hips and began to squeak.

"Everyone listen to me!" Sweet Pea shouted in her loudest voice. "We all need to get a grip. I know its Squishmas and we're all very excited, especially about the Wishy Squishy Soup, but we are making too much noise and being a little unkind to one another. It's making me more than upset, so I have decided in my best thinking hat that we are going to do the Squish and Pop dance!"

"Yay! I love the Squish and Pop dance," shouted Winkers.

"Me too, me too, me too!" cried all the little Squishes and Squashes.

Sweet Pea finally had their attention. She climbed a small wooden ladder which took her to a

"Yay! I love the Squish and Pop dance."

Look at Grandma dance

pocket sized stage covered in tinsel and fairy lights, giving her a more than perfect setting to perform the dance. Sweet Pea began to move from side to side and then started to make a square shape on the ground with her feet. It wasn't long till all the little Squishes and Squashes joined in, each of them grinning ear-to-ear. The Squish and Pop dance was actually quite complicated which meant the little squirrels had to focus on what they were doing. It worked in calming the excited little squirrels down.

"Oooooooooh!" said Grandpa Squish. "Look at you squishing and popping!" Grandpa Squish watched Grandma Squash proudly as she executed the movement with oodles of awesomeness.

Grandma Squash used to be a professional hip-hop dancer, so it was a sight to see her performing the routine.

Clearly outdone by Grandma Squash's performance, all the little Squishes and Squashes sat down to listen to Grandpa Squish's Squishmas Eve story.

Well almost all of them. Sweet Pea had seen the snow clouds outside and was waiting rather impatiently for them to blow their kisses. When the snow clouds get full in Squishville, they blow kisses. The kisses are tiny heart-shaped snowflakes and each one has its own unique pattern.

The little snowflakes create a loving blanket of snow. The snow in Squishville is different to the snow you might know – when you touch it, it feels warm and it glows orange. It sends warmth to your heart and your cheeks turn rosy, just like big cherries. This special snow fills the air with a sweet smell of waffles and maple syrup.

Once Sweet Pea had seen the snow clouds blow their kisses she quickly sat down.

Sweet Pea watched the snow clouds

The Squishes and Squashes weren't upset that Sweet Pea had made story time a little late for them. It made them all so happy to see Sweet Pea enjoying the snow kisses so much.

Chapter Two

Sparkle Stars

The magical Sparkle Stars

Grandpa Squish started to speak, "Now, before I tell my story I would like to know what everyone's most favourite part of Squishmas is."

The little Squishes and Squashes filled up with excitement once again, so much so it looked like they were all going to pop!

"I like all the yummy things we get to eat at Squishmas time, Grandpa Squish, although I am not

really sure which is my favourite because they all taste soooooo nice. But I especially like the Ping-Pong Mops this time of year," said Sausage Pot.

"OOOOOH, OOOOOH, OOOOH, me, me!" shouted Tiddlypops.

"Ah, little Tiddlypops, what is your favourite part?" asked Grandpa Squish.

"Well, there are so many parts I like about Squishmas, but my most favourite part is the Wishy Squishy Soup that Grandma Squash makes," said Tiddlypops.

The room was filled with even more excitement as Tiddlypops reminded all of the other little Squishes and Squashes about this special bit of Squishmas magic.

"OOOOOOOH I love the Wishy Squishy Soup too," said Sweet Pea, bouncing up and down.

"Me too!" said Binky Bonk and Stinky Stonk at the same time.

All the other little Squishes and Squashes agreed.

"Hang on," said Sausage Pot as he was eating one of Grandma Squash's Cherry Bake Cakes. "Where is Grandma Squash?"

The little Squishes and Squashes looked around and were very concerned because they couldn't see Grandma Squash. Sweet Pea was just about to cry when Grandpa Squish said, "Don't you remember, little Squishes and Squashes? What does Grandma Squash do on Squishmas Eve?"

"Ah I know, I know, I know," said Windipops as he let a few air bubbles out of his bottom. "She goes and talks to the Sparkle Stars in the ground because she thinks they get lonely."

"No, no," said Winkers batting his eyelashes. "She talks to the Sparkle Stars to tell them what a good job they are doing and that she is grateful to them because they make us all very happy."

"And that she loves them, with all of her squishy squashy heart," said Bibbibob Bits as all of his things fell out of his pocket.

"Yes, that's right little Squishes and Squashes," said Grandpa Squish.

Grandma Squish talks to the Sparkle Stars

"Grandpa Squish, if you tell things that you really, really love them, do they grow big and strong?" asked Bibbibob Bits.

"Yes they do," said Grandpa Squish as he looked out of the snow-covered window to see Grandma Squash talking warmly to the Sparkle Stars. "If you show love and give love to something it can only grow in a happy way."

"Wow, that's so cool. So if I tell my tiny plants and my fish, Gary, how much I love them everyday they will grow huge and happy?" asked Bibbibob Bits.

"Well I am not sure how big they will grow but they will definitely be happy," said Grandpa Squish with a huge grin spreading across his round furry face.

All the little Squishes and Squashes then ran towards one of the snow-covered windows where they could see Grandma Squash talking kindly to the magical Sparkle Stars. It was nearly time for the little Stars to pop up and burst out from the ground, turning all the wishes in the little squirrels' heads into real ones.

Squatipops could see that poor old Tiddlypops could not see out of the window because he was far too small, so he picked his best friend up by his blue shiny cape.

Tiddlypops looked out of the window

All the Squishes and Squashes huddled around the fire

"Thank you Squatipops," said Tiddlypops.

"Now, shall we get back to my Squishmas story?" laughed Grandpa Squish. All the little Squishes and Squashes scurried back and huddled together on their stools to make a squirrel-bodied heart shape on the rug in front of the warm, cosy fire.

"Now, I've got a special surprise for you all today. My story is actually about the Sparkle Stars!" said Grandpa Squish.

"Yay!" cheered the little squirrels."

"Grandpa Squish, this is going to be the best

Squishmas story ever. I can't wait! Oooooh! Grandpa Squish, please tell the story," blurted out Sweet Pea.

"I think that is what Grandpa Squish is trying to do, Sweet Pea," said Tiddlypops.

The little Squishes and Squashes could not believe how lucky they were. They quickly settled down to make sure they had all eyes and ears on Grandpa Squish's story.

They all listened to Grandpa Squish's story

Chapter Three

Storytime

Grandpa Squish tells a story

"It was the day before Squishmas and I was taking one of my wonderful wobbly walks through the village which always fills me with gratitude. The snow clouds had blown their kisses and the ground was covered in a soft sheet of magic. The little Squishes and Squashes were wrapped tightly in their warm, winter clothes giving even more colour to this most enchanted village.

As I looked over to our mushroom house, which was covered in a mountain of snow, I noticed lots of squirrels gathering around our back garden.

I could see the smaller Squishes and Squashes at the back of the crowd trying to jump up and down so they could see."

"See what?" shouted Tiddlypops

"The Sparkle Stars of course," said Sweet Pea.

"Oh yeah… OOOOOOH Sparkle Stars, Sparkle Stars," Tiddlypops was overcome with so much excitement he almost grew a little bit.

"Yes, they were all watching Grandma Squash talk to the Sparkle Stars and they wanted to see how big the Sparkle Stars had grown. Some say that when the Sparkle Stars grow to a certain point just

before they pop out of the ground, they talk to Grandma Squash," said Grandpa Squish.

"About what?" shouted Binky Bonk and Stinky Stonk at the same time.

"I bet they tell Grandma Squash what a wonderful person she is and thank her for all the love she gives them to help them grow into big wishes," said Tiddlypops.

Every little Squish and Squash turned towards Tiddlypops and cheered.

"Yes, little Tiddlypops, I think you might be right," said Grandpa Squish.

"Can you eat the Sparkle Stars, Grandpa Squish?" said Sausage Pot.

No!" shouted all the little Squishes and Squashes as they looked at Sausage Pot with very upset faces.

"Ok I was just checking. You never know – they might taste like chocolate," said Sausage Pot as he sunk back into his stool.

"It was now Squishmas morning, and what a beautiful morning it was. The warm glowing lights shone from the snow-covered windows of our wonderful little mushroom houses." said Grandpa Squish.

"You could hear the excited squeaks and squirks coming from inside each house, wishes of "Happy Squishmas!" and the sound of warm fires crackling.

The warm air rose up through the heart-shaped chimneys making heart-shaped patterns in the orange sky. It was without a doubt Squishmas in Squishville, a very special day.

Grandma Squash was already up – in fact, I don't think she went to sleep at all. I could hear a lot of magical sounds coming from the kitchen. Grandma Squash was singing very loudly. You see, Grandma Squash is deaf in one ear so sometimes she doesn't know how loud she is. This means a lot of our neighbours get to hear all her wonderful sounds too!"

All the little Squishes and Squashes smiled warmly from one fuzzy cheek to the other as Grandpa Squish continued to tell his story.

"I made my way down the steep wooden stairs which were lit by the smallest of fairy lights and was greeted with a cup of Grandma Squash's super-duper, Hot Chocolate Surprise.

It's called a Surprise because no one knows quite what goes into this special recipe and it's always surprisingly different," said Grandpa Squish.

"Super-duper Hot Chocolate Surprise," said Sausage pot as he licked his lips and rubbed his tummy.

All the little Squishes and Squashes squiggled and giggled at Sausage Pot rubbing his tummy.

"Why does Grandma Squash wake up so early Grandpa Squish?" said Tiddlypops.

"Grandma Squash gets up so early as she likes to decorate the whole mushroom house for Squishmas. Every part of our mushroom house is covered from ear to feet in sparkles and sprinkles just like it is today." said Grandpa Squish.

"It makes me smile so much when I see the decorations, Grandpa Squish. It makes me feel warm and tingly inside," said Tiddlypops.

"And me," said Windipops.

"And me," said Winkers.

"And me," said Sausage Pot.

"And me," said the rest of the little Squishes and Squashes.

"And that is why Grandma Squash does it, because she knows how happy it makes you all," said Grandpa Squish. Then Sausage Pot burped so loud that it made all the little Squishes and Squashes laugh and Grandpa Squish was able to get back to his story.

The Squishes and Squashes made their wishes

"So, it was time for all the little Squishes and Squashes to get their special cup of Wishy Squishy Soup. They were called up one-by-one and each made their wishes. The wishes then floated up the heart-shaped chimney and into the Squishmas sky.

Once the little squirrels had made their wishes and eaten their magical soup, off they went to join their fuzzy families in their own mushroom houses for more fun and games.

When all the Squishes and Squashes had gone, I sat with Grandma Squash and drank another cup of super-duper Hot Chocolate Surprise.

As we sat happily on our stools thinking about all the wonderful wishes that had been made, we could hear a noise coming from the fireplace.

Grandma Squash wobbled over to where the sound was coming from. As she looked up the chimney she could see there was a tiny wish floating halfway up.

"Oh dear," said Grandma Squash.

"What is it Grandma Squash?" I replied.

"There is a wish stuck halfway up the chimney," said Grandma Squash in a very worried voice.

Chapter Four

Who's Wish

"Oh no! We need to find out who it belongs to soon, before the night sky and the sleepy stars come in. Grandma Squash was so overcome with upset she froze. There was no time for me to give Grandma Squash a long, warm hug to snap her out of it so out I went into Squishville walking as fast as I could through the snow kisses and knocked on every single mushroom-house door.

I asked each little Squish and Squash if they all wished with all their hearts on their magical Sparkle Stars, and each one of them said, "Yes, of course!" and asked if they should make a second wish just to make sure. But I decided that this was not necessary."

"Oh no, Grandpa Squish! I hope you found the little Squish or Squash it belonged to," said Sweet Pea.

"Well, Sweet Pea, then I remembered earlier when Grandma Squash was handing out the Wishy Squishy Soup that I saw a little Squash moving towards the door. I asked her if she was ok and she said she just needed to get some air," said Grandpa Squish.

"OOOOH she could have had some of mine," said Windipops.

"I don't think she wanted that sort of air, Windipops," said Sausage Pot.

All the little Squishes and Squashes squiggled and giggled.

"This little Squash was called Pottypops. So I quickly made my way through the snow clouds to Pottypops' mushroom house, and as the door opened I was met by Pottypops' mummy. Mummy Pops greeted me with a warm smile and a big hug. I could see some little eyes peering from around a great big tail, which made the little Squash look even smaller."

I said, "We have a bit of a problem, one of the wishes has got stuck in the chimney."

"Oh dear," said Mummy Pops. "Do you want me to help you save it?"

"The only way we can do that is to find the little Squish or Squash that made the wish. You see, in order for the wishes to come true, you have to truly believe in them. The only reason for the wish to be stuck is that it wasn't wished on properly. Pottypops pulled further into her mummy's tail and completely disappeared. I continued to talk.

"The problem is, if there is one Sparkle Star that wasn't wished on properly then all the other wishes won't come true."

Pottypops slowly emerged from her mummy's fluffy tail and looked at me with huge sad eyes.

"I am sorry, Grandpa Squish, it was me. I didn't wish properly. I didn't believe that my wish could come true because it was so big," said Pottypops.

Pottypops was afraid

"So big? Why, little Pottypops dear, it doesn't matter how big the wish is as long as you wish for it with your whole heart," I replied.

"Deep in my heart I knew that, Grandpa Squish, but I was scared of making the wish just in case it didn't come true and I would be upset. I was afraid," said Pottypops.

"That's ok to feel like that little Pottypops. We all feel like that sometimes, we just have to take a great big gulp, be brave and make that wish with all our heart."

Within a second, Pottypops had bounced onto my shoulders and off we went with Mummy Pops to save her wish.

Chapter Five

Save the Wish

A wish was stuck in the chimney

As we entered our mushroom house I realised I'd forgotten about poor old Grandma Squash and she was still standing there, frozen to the spot. I don't know how she managed it but she was now in a headstand. So I tickled her toes and she quickly snapped out of it and starting pouring a special cup of...

"The WISH!!!" she shouted as she remembered what had happened.

"It's ok, Grandma Squash," I said. "We know who the wish belongs to and Pottypops here is going to rescue everyone's wish by being strong and brave."

Little Pottypops quickly scurried over to the fireplace, her tiny squirrel body glowing in front of the fire as she looked up the tall, stone chimney.

Pottypops sang a little wish song

"OOOOOH WISH, I am so sorry for not believing in you. You are such a strong and brave wish I know you can fly as high as the sleepy stars and the smiling moon. So, I am going to make my wish again," whispered Pottypops.

Little Pottypops closed her eyes tight and sang a little wish song:

And without any time for the big wish to stay,
The wish floated up, up all the way.
It went through the chimney as quiet as a mouse
Floated up to the sky to find its new house.

In the dark sleepy night that lay quiet and calm,
The strong little wish threw out both its arms,
And gave it a hug as big as the moon,
'Twas so glad to be there, it sang a small tune,
And set every wish free to float up and stay,
And there grew the wishes, bigger each day!

"Yippee!" cried Grandma Squash."

Mummy Pops picked up little Pottypops and gave her the biggest squash ever.

"And yes, all the little Squishes and Squashes wishes came true," said Grandpa Squish with joy.

"Wow, Grandpa Squish, I think this is my favourite story ever!" squeaked Tiddlypops.

"So, Grandpa Squish, if you don't believe in wishes enough then they don't come true?" asked Sweet Pea.

"Yes, Sweet Pea, you have to believe them with your whole heart," said Grandpa Squish.

"What about Tiddlypops? His head and heart are so small, will he be big enough to make a wish come true?" asked Windipops.

"Well, Tiddlypops has more power in his little body than you can imagine," said Grandpa Squish.

Tiddlypops then gave a small smile as he looked kindly upon Grandpa Squish.

"And do I get more wishes because I am a bit bigger than most Squishes and Squashes, Grandpa Squish?" said Sausage Pot.

"No, Sausage Pot, it doesn't quite work like that," said Grandpa Squish.

"Ah that's a shame, 'cause I could have wished for more of Grandma Squash's Cherry Bake Cakes," said Sausage Pot.

The little Squishes and Squashes were filled with so much warmth that a soft orange light glowed around their little squirrel bodies. The light shone through the windows of the mushroom house, right up to the snow clouds, lighting up the clear night sky.

The light shone through the windows

"Now it is time for you all to get some rest, to make sure you are all bright-eyed and bushy-tailed to make your wishes tomorrow. Good night, little Squishes and Squashes," said Grandpa Squish.

They would see all their wishes come true

"Good night, Grandpa Squish. Good night, Grandma Squash," said all the little Squishes and Squashes.

And off they scurried, knowing that the next morning they would get to wish upon the magical Sparkle Stars and see all their wishes come true.

We wish you a very Merry Squishmas, and hope you get to make a wish on this most special of days.

Hope to see you soon, here in Squishville.

The End

The Most Top Secret Squirrel Mission

SHHHHHH!

You must tell absolutely NO ONE about this secret mission!

It is MOST TOP SECRET!

Once completed you can tell your family and friends and help them through the mission.

Turn over for all SECRET squirrel instructions.

Do this quietly (SHHHHH) It needs to be a secret even from your pets!

The Mission

Your mission is to daydream.

About what?

About things that make you happy.

Why?

Because the more time you spend thinking about the things that make you happy, the more happy things will be present in your life.

Why does this happen?

We are all energy and we attract things we think about most. Think of yourself like a magnet, the thoughts in your head make electrical conversations with the universe, so the better thoughts you have in your head the better things will be.

Little Tip

If you ever feel sad, think of something that makes you happy. You could also try singing as this sends vibrations all the way around your body which makes you feel happier.

Dancing is good too!

Ps. Don't worry if you're not the best singer or dancer in the world, it still works the same.

My Thank You's

I would like to say a huge big thank you to Ann Foo for all of her wonderful illustrations in the book.

A big round of applause to my gorgeous niece Lilly Foo Black for helping me find some of my favourite squirrels.

To Lisa Edwards for your excellent copy-editing skills.

And a HUGE squishy squashy thank you to Clive Ketteridge for believing in Squishville.

Not to forget the HUGE support of my wonderful family and friends.

Great BIG LOVE to you all.......

About the Author

I found Squishville while walking in the woods at the end of my garden one morning, I was so inspired by this enchanted little village that I wanted to share it with you.

I believe that there are lots of secret magic places hidden in the world that have yet to be discovered, you might even have one in your garden! The secret in finding one is to always be on the look out for magic, as it may lie in the places you least expect.

Taira Foo is an emerging author of children's books. This book follows the first in the series ' Welcome to Squishville.'

Always look for the magic, as it may be right beside you

....

Made in United States
Troutdale, OR
12/11/2024

26334896R00031